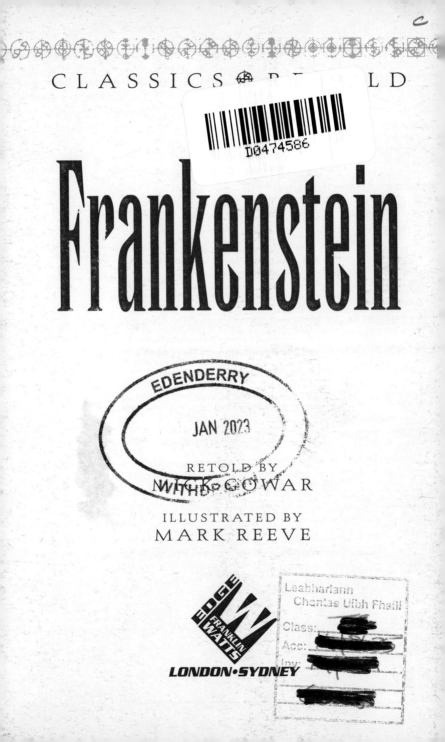

CLASSICS RETOLD

Frankenstein

RETOLD BY
MICK GOWAR

ILLUSTRATED BY
MARK REEVE

EDGE
FRANKLIN WATTS

LONDON·SYDNEY

First published in 2011 by
Franklin Watts
338 Euston Road
London NW1 3BH

Franklin Watts Australia
Level 17/207 Kent Street
Sydney NSW 2000

Text © Franklin Watts 2011
Illustrations by Mark Reeve © Franklin Watts 2011
Cover design by Peter Scoulding

Picture acknowledgements: Cover: Istockphoto © Shannon Toth;
Shutterstock © DGDesign; p.46 © Classic Collection/Alamy

A CIP catalogue record for this book
is available from the British Library.

ISBN: 978 1 4451 0458 4

Dewey Classification: 823.9'14

3 5 7 9 10 8 6 4 2

Printed in Great Britain

Franklin Watts is a division of Hachette Children's Books,
an Hachette UK company.
www.hachette.co.uk

Contents

Chapter One
A mysterious traveller

On a wintry afternoon in October 1797, Captain Robert Walton and his sister Mrs Margaret Seville met for the first time in two years. The Captain had just returned from a long and dangerous voyage to the Arctic Sea and he had an incredible story to tell.

'We were sailing north towards Iceland when our ship became jammed in some pack ice. The temperature dropped and the sea froze fast around us. The ship was trapped like a twig in a frozen pond. Freezing fog surrounded us and we could see nothing for miles. All we could hear was the ice cracking and groaning.

When at last the fog lifted, it was late afternoon. I gazed out through my telescope to see if there was any break in the ice. I saw a sledge, pulled by dogs, hurtling across the ice. It was being driven by a giant! I was close enough to hear his whip cracking and the dogs barking, and I could see that the driver was more than eight feet tall. He steered the sledge around a mound of ice and vanished.

The next morning, I was woken early by the excited shouts of the crew. I pulled on my thick fur coat and hurried up the icy wooden steps to the deck. The ice around the ship had cracked and melted a little in the night so the ship was floating freely. On one icy island was a broken dog sledge. Hunched beside it was a man dressed in thick furs. Only one dog was still alive, huddled against its master.

The ice block floated closer until it was nearly touching the side of the ship. This man was not the giant I had seen the day before. This man was small, hunched over and exhausted. He looked like a broken puppet.

My crew called out to him. The man looked up.

"Where are you going?" he cried. "I must go north. If you are headed north, please take me with you."

We threw a rope down to him, but he was too weak to climb it. Instead, my crew climbed down and carried the man and his dog across the ice and onto the ship. They carried him below deck and laid him on my bunk. I covered him with as many blankets as I could find. He was so cold and still that I thought he must be dead, but after a moment, the man stirred and groaned.

"Bring some hot soup to warm this poor man up!" I called to my crew.

A young deckhand brought me some soup. I sat beside the man and lifted a spoonful to his mouth. Slowly, he began to sip. After a few spoonfuls, he struggled to sit up.

"Lie down." I told him. "Rest."

But the man struggled again to sit up.

"I—I must tell my story," he said. "I am dying, but I must warn you, warn the whole world of what I have done."

Again, I tried to make him lie down and rest, but he would not. He was determined to speak, even if it killed him.

Chapter Two
The young scientist

In a weak voice, the man told me that his name was Victor Frankenstein. His father was a baron and their family home was a castle in Switzerland, near Geneva.

Victor's parents were good and kind people. On their travels, they met a poor little orphan girl. They decided to adopt her and brought her up alongside Victor. Her name was Elizabeth. Years later, they had another son. They named him William.

When Victor was 17, Elizabeth fell gravely ill with a fever. Victor's mother nursed

Elizabeth back to health, but in doing so, caught the fever herself and died a few days later. On her deathbed, she told Victor and Elizabeth that her dearest wish had been to see them marry one day.

In his grief, Victor threw himself into his studies. On summer days when Elizabeth and Henry, Victor's best friend, played ball in the sunshine or fished in the lake, Victor was indoors, hidden in a dark corner of the castle library. In that corner were ancient books. Books that told of wise men who did strange experiments. Men who spent years

trying to turn ordinary metals into the one metal that would never rust, never tarnish: gold. The wise men's aim was not to become rich, but to create something perfect. They believed that men and women could be made perfect, too.

As Victor travelled around Geneva in the family carriage, he saw poor people sitting by the road. They were unable to walk and were begging because they could get no work. Victor decided to devote his life to healing people like them. When he was 18 he went to university to become a doctor.

One of Victor's teachers at university was Professor Krempe. He reminded Victor of a fox – sharp-nosed and sharp-tongued.

During his training, Victor told Professor Krempe about the books he'd read in the castle library. Krempe snorted with disgust.

"Magic! Superstition! Nonsense! Those wise men weren't scientists. They were fakes, conjurors!" He scribbled some words on a piece of paper, screwed the paper into a ball and threw it at Victor.

"There! Buy and read those books. And burn those books of nonsense you've been reading."

Victor did as he was told. But the strange ideas stayed in his mind. As he learned more about modern science, such as how the nerves and blood vessels work, what makes the heart beat and the limbs move, Victor made a promise to himself. He would use his new knowledge to create life. He would make the perfect man!

Chapter Three
The new Prometheus

There was once a Greek god called Prometheus. He crafted the first humans out of mud and brought them to life. Over time, Prometheus grew fond of his creations and he stole food and fire from the gods to feed and warm them. But Prometheus was found out and he was harshly punished by the mighty god Zeus. He was chained to a rock, and every day an eagle pecked out his liver.

Like Prometheus, Victor believed that he could bring a man to life. But he never thought about how he might be punished.

Creating the perfect creature was not a perfect business. Victor haunted the university's medical school dissecting rooms. He hid in cupboards waiting for the professors and students to leave. Then he would creep out to steal parts for his creature: hands from one body; kidneys from another; a heart from a third.

But piecing together the tiny blood vessels, joining the nerves was fiddly and difficult. So Victor decided to make his creature bigger – around eight feet tall. It took hours of painstaking work to stitch all the pieces together. Victor became so absorbed in his work that he didn't eat or sleep for days at a

at a time. He became thinner and thinner.
His eyes sunk back into his head. As the
creature grew, so Victor was turning into
a corpse.

After months of work, Victor's creation was
ready. The creature lay in a bath filled with
chemicals. Attached to the creature's limbs
and running up into the roof were long
lengths of copper wire. All Victor's creation
needed now was a spark of electricity to
bring it to life: lightning!

Victor paced up and down. There was no
sign of a storm. One day passed. Then a
second. Victor dared not sit down. He knew
he would fall asleep, and if he fell asleep, he
might miss that one precious moment.

On the third night, the wind began to
ripple the heavy curtains beside Victor's

open window. Rain began to fall, at first slowly, then quicker and quicker. Thunder clouds began to mass above the house. From far in the distance came a low rumble.

Victor counted: "One... two... three... four... five." Then came a faint, milky lightening of the sky.

"Five miles away," muttered Victor.

There was another rumble of thunder.

"One... two... three..." The sky brightened. Then darkness again. Then came a crack, followed almost at once by a blinding flash.

Boom! went the thunder. "Now!" shouted Victor. "Now!"

A blazing ribbon of lightning shot across the night sky and down to the roof of the building. Victor could suddenly smell burning. The creature began to stir.

There was another flash of lightning. Victor could at last see his creation in the bright light. He gave a cry of horror. He could see the creature clearly, and it wasn't beautiful at all, it was hideous!

Victor held up a candle. The creature cringed and backed away. It was a monster! Its skin was yellow and pulled tight across its bones and muscles, so that every scar was a shining white stripe across its face and body. Its eyes were bloodshot and its lips were raw gashes across its hideous face. Its enormous size only made it look more monstrous, like a raw wound under a magnifying glass.

With a cry, Victor ran from the room and stumbled down the narrow stairs, past the locked doors of the other people who lived in the building. He pushed open the front door and staggered out into the rain. He fell onto the wet cobbles of the street, at the feet of a man wrapped in a thick cloak.

"Help me!" Victor gasped.

"Victor!" exclaimed the muffled figure. "Whatever is the matter?" It was Henry Clerval, Victor's childhood friend. "I haven't heard from you in months. I came to see if anything was the matter. What is it, Victor? What on Earth has happened?"

But Victor didn't answer. He lay unconscious at Henry's feet.

Chapter Four
The monster strikes

Henry managed to half drag, half carry Victor back to his own lodgings. He put Victor in his bed. Henry slept in an armchair, forcing a sip of water or a spoonful of soup between Victor's lips whenever he stirred. It took weeks before Victor was fully conscious. He was weak and pale, but well enough to travel. Victor and Henry decided to journey to the nearby mountains for some fresh air.

After a few weeks, Victor began to recover. He was confident the monster must be dead. There was no news of an eight-foot-tall creature being seen. It would not be able to speak, so it wouldn't be able to ask for help, or food, or clothes or shelter. Without shelter or food it could not live. It was enormous, but it was as helpless as a newborn baby.

"Forget the monster," Victor said to himself. "It must be dead."

Then a letter arrived from his father. Terrible news. His younger brother William was dead, horribly murdered. As he read the letter, Victor's heart pounded and he began to sweat.

The family maid, Justine, had been found sleeping near the body. She had been arrested and charged with the murder. The police said she killed William in a fit of madness. Only a mad-woman, they said, could have killed young William so brutally. And in Geneva there was only one punishment for a murderer: death! A fever of guilt and horror made Victor sick and dizzy. He knew at once who the murderer really was: the monster. The thing was still alive.

Victor ran as fast as he could to Henry's room. He pounded on the door.

"Henry, I beg you, open up. Quickly! We must hire a coach and ride to Geneva – now! One life is lost already, and another is in grave danger!"

Victor and Henry arrived in Geneva the next morning and hurried to the courthouse. In the dock stood Justine. She tried to explain that she had been sleeping while William was killed, but the judge did not believe her.

Victor sat in the court in agony. "I must

say something," he muttered to himself. "But what? If I tell the judge I created a monster he won't believe me. If I tell him I know my monster killed William, he'll say I'm mad. He'll lock me up forever. Oh, what can I do? What can I say?"

Victor sat hunched miserably in his seat. The judge banged his gavel on the bench.

"Silence! I sentence the prisoner... to death!" he boomed.

There was murmur of approval from the spectators.

Victor put his head in his hands.

The day Justine was executed, Victor collapsed and was carried to bed. Once again Henry, and this time Elizabeth, nursed him. After several weeks he was well enough to take a holiday in the mountains.

"The mountain air will do him good," said Henry. "It helped when he was ill before."

Victor's father agreed. "But no climbing or long walks," he warned.

"Come back soon, dear Victor," said Elizabeth. "I will miss you so much."

Chapter Five
A monstrous bride

After a week in the mountains, Victor was strong enough to take a short walk alone. But as he walked slowly up the steep path Victor saw a shadow on the slope above him. It was the shadow of an enormous man. Victor hurried up the slope and around a corner, and there stood the monster, sitting on a rock waiting for him.

"You!" gasped Victor. "You murdered my brother."

"I did," said the monster. "But you abandoned me! How could you? I am your creation, your child."

"You are no child of mine!" cried Victor. "You are hideous, evil; a monster! I should destroy you now." He raised his walking stick. The creature grabbed it and, with his powerful hands, snapped the sturdy stick in two.

The creature glared at him. "I am as you made me. I was helpless and you ran from me. I needed you and you left me. I had to steal these poor rags I am wearing. I had to steal food. I had to steal water. If I hadn't stolen I would have died. I tried to ask for help. But whenever I approached anyone they screamed and ran from me – as you did – or they beat me without mercy. The first words I learnt were curses: Monster! Devil!"

The creature went on. "After my last beating I travelled far into the country, moving by night. I crept from barn to barn. I stole eggs from hen houses. Sometimes I trapped a rabbit or squirrel, and ate it raw. After many weeks, I found a ruined shed by a tiny cottage. A family lived in the cottage: a blind father and his son and daughter. Good, kind people. I ate the few crusts, vegetable peelings, scraps of meat and cheese they threw away. Through a hole in the thin

wall I watched the family. That's how I
learned to speak. I listened to the family and
copied their words, whispering them to
myself over and over when the family slept.

Then one day, when the son and daughter were out in the fields, I knocked at the cottage door. The blind father let me in and gave me food. We talked happily, until his son and daughter returned. One look at me and the daughter fainted. The gentle son took a stick and beat me until I ran from the cottage."

"So I decided to come looking for you, my creator. I had heard the family talk of a nearby town called Geneva, and it seemed like a good place to start looking for you. I made my way slowly towards it. I travelled only by night and used the stars as my guide. Eventually I came to Geneva and found your family's home. I made a hiding place in the woods nearby and waited. And it was there your brother found me. I didn't mean to harm him, but he saw me and screamed. He screamed and screamed and screamed. I only squeezed his throat to stop him."

The monster hid his enormous face in his hands. Then he looked at Victor.

"Make me a companion, as you made me. Someone who will not scream or beat me. Make me a wife and I will disappear. I'll go far away from men and women, I swear. Otherwise, I will haunt you all your life, Victor Frankenstein. I will never leave you in peace!"

Victor recoiled in horror, and fled back down the mountain. Henry was sitting in the hotel, drinking hot chocolate. Victor burst in, his eyes wild with fear.

"Victor!" said Henry. "What is the matter?"

"I need your help," said Victor. "We must leave here at once."

"Why?" asked Henry. "What's happened?"

"I can't tell you," said Victor. "Just please trust me Henry."

Victor and Henry returned to Geneva. They told Victor's father the sea air was what Victor needed to make him well again. Victor promised Elizabeth that when he returned, they would marry. Tears and happy laughter sped them on their way.

Henry and Victor travelled north by coach, then sailed across the stormy North Sea to Scotland. From there they travelled further north to the far-off Orkney Islands.

Chapter Six
A cruel blow

Henry found them rooms at a small hotel, but Victor would not stay. He left Henry at the hotel and rented a cottage far from prying eyes. There he began to create a new creature – a wife for his monster. But as he worked, Victor was sure that someone was watching him. Glancing up from his bench, Victor sometimes glimpsed a huge shadow that quickly vanished into the darkness.

Months passed. The new creature was almost finished when Victor realised he had made a terrible mistake.

"It's madness to create another monster!" he said to himself. "A wife for a monster! What if they have children? I will have created a race of evil creatures! No! I must destroy it!"

Taking a scalpel and saw he began to take his creation apart. As he chopped, Victor heard a sound from outside – a mixture of a sob and a howl. He looked up. A huge shadow blocked the window.

"You have cheated me Frankenstein!" howled the creature. "You have killed my wife and I will take my revenge. I will curse *your* wedding night! You will pay for this."

Victor ran to the door and flung it open. All he saw was an enormous shadow disappearing along the path. He ran down the sloping path to the hotel where Henry was staying, his heart pounding with fear. Before he turned the corner, Victor heard screams. The landlord was outside holding a blazing torch. The other guests stood in the road. The landlord pointed to a huge figure scrambling up the hillside behind the hotel with superhuman speed.

"There he goes – the murderer!"

"Who is murdered?" gasped Victor.

"Oh, sir," the landlord hesitated. "Your friend. Murdered by that –" he pointed up the hill. But the monster had vanished into the darkness.

Chapter Seven
Victor's wedding

Years passed. Over time, Victor gradually learned to live with the loss of his best friend. Then one sunny spring day in Geneva, he finally married his childhood sweetheart, Elizabeth.

That evening, Victor and his new bride returned to the hotel where they were to spend their wedding night.

"Victor, this has been the happiest day of my life," Elizabeth beamed. Her smile faded. "If only William and Henry could have been here to share our joy."

Victor sighed. "My dear," he said. "I fear that the same evil thing that killed William and Henry will try to kill me tonight."

Elizabeth stared at Victor, wide-eyed.

"Don't worry, my dear, I have these." Victor drew two pistols from his pocket and laid them on the table beside the bed. "And this." He pulled aside his jacket. Hanging from his belt was a sword. "I have booked an extra bedroom, next door. Go there and lock the door. Don't unlock it unless you hear my voice. Do you understand?"

Elizabeth nodded.

"Go now, before darkness comes," said Victor.

Elizabeth kissed him. "Be careful, my darling," she said. But Victor was already staring out of the open window, looking for the moving shadow he knew was out there, somewhere, getting closer.

Victor waited. One hour, two hours, three. Still no sign of the monster. "Where are you?" muttered Victor. "I remember your promise. I'm ready for you!"

There was a crash of breaking glass, but it didn't come from the window in front of him. It came from the room next door. There was a scream, suddenly cut off. Then silence.

Victor ran into the corridor. Elizabeth's door was still locked. He threw himself at it. The lock broke and the door flew open. On the bed lay Elizabeth. Victor let out a cry like a wounded beast. The monster had cursed his wedding night. Elizabeth, his lovely bride, was dead.

Chapter Eight
The final pursuit

Victor Frankenstein left the hotel that night determined to catch and kill the monster. He would finally put an end to all the misery it had caused. He would not rest until the monster, or he, was dead.

He followed the monster across Germany on horseback. He followed it across Russia by coach and sleigh. Finally, he chased it across the frozen sea on a dog sledge.

Victor gradually closed the gap between him and the monster. At one point, the monster was less than a mile away in the distance. Victor urged his weary dogs on. But suddenly, the ice sheet beneath him cracked and set him adrift on the icy sea. All but one of his team of dogs died, one by one, and Victor himself was close to starvation when he glimpsed our ship on the horizon.

As he finished his story, Victor struggled to sit up in my bunk. "Captain Walton, you must take me further north after the creature. I must destroy it!"

I shook my head. "We must go back south. The ice is too thick for my ship, there is no way through."

Victor clutched at me, but the effort was too much for him. With a gasp, he fell back on the bunk, dead.

Sadly, I pulled the sheet over his face, and climbed the steps to the deck. I needed to find my first officer. We had to bury Victor here, at sea, as soon as the ice melted. But before I could speak I heard a crash from below.

I ran down the steps. The porthole of my cabin had been smashed open and there stood an enormous creature. It could only be Victor's monster. He turned to face me. On his hideous face was a look of great sadness.

"It is done," he said in a harsh voice. "My creator is dead. All that is left for me is to die, too. There is no place for me in your world, even in this wilderness."

He leapt through the porthole. I watched as the enormous figure jumped from ice floe to ice floe until it vanished into the darkness.'

Captain Walton had finally finished telling his story. He took a deep breath, and settled back in his armchair.

His sister looked back at him, her mouth open. There was a long silence. Then she spoke, her words coming slowly:

"Well, Robert. I must say, that is a frightful story."

Mary Shelley (1797—1851)

Mary Shelley was born on 30 August, 1797 in London to Mary Wollstonecraft, a famous feminist, and William Godwin, a political writer. Mary's mother died just ten days after giving birth, leaving William to bring up his daughter alone.

Mary Shelley

Mary grew up surrounded by poets and writers, many of whom visited her father regularly. At the age of 16, she ran away with the poet Percy Shelley, who was six years older than her and already married. They fled to Europe, where they spent the next few years travelling. In 1816, Percy's wife Harriet killed herself, and Percy and Mary married. They settled in Italy.

During this time, they both wrote what is thought of as their best work. Their brief marriage was dogged with tragedy though. Three of their children died in childbirth, and Percy himself was drowned in 1822 when the boat he was travelling in capsized.

Mary dedicated the rest of her life to her one surviving son, Percy, and to writing.

Frankenstein (1818)

The story behind *Frankenstein* is almost as interesting as the book itself. During the summer of 1816, Mary, Percy and a friend, poet Lord Byron, were staying beside Lake Geneva in Switzerland. One evening, they decided to write ghost stories. Mary struggled at first, until she had a terrifying dream where she witnessed the meeting between the monster and his creator. She immediately started writing the book that was to become *Frankenstein*.

Titles in the CLASSICS RETOLD series:

978 0 4451 0461 4
Ebook edition: 978 1 4451 0818 6

978 0 4451 0460 7
Ebook edition: 978 1 4451 0815 5

978 0 4451 0458 4
Ebook edition: 978 1 4451 0819 3

978 0 4451 0462 1
Ebook edition: 978 1 4451 0817 9

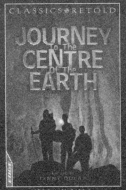

978 0 4451 0459 1
Ebook edition: 978 1 4451 0816 2

978 0 4451 0459 1
Ebook edition: 978 1 4451 0816 2